THE Sea

THE Sea

PIRET RAUD

The Sea loved her fish very much.

She looked after them the best she could –
fed and bathed them, took them for a walk in the park...

...and read them a bedtime story.

But sometimes the Sea grew tired and was sad –
for example, when she wanted some peace and quiet
to think her own thoughts but couldn't, because the
fish were shouting and misbehaving.

In these moments, the Sea stared at the clouds
gliding in the sky and longed to be somewhere else.
Somewhere it was silent. Where there were no fish.

One day, when the fish were being especially loud,
it happened. The Sea got fed up and left.

She simply went away! Without the fish!

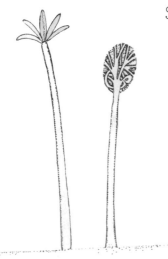

At first, the fish were not at all bothered.
They were even pleased that the Sea
was away. They joked around...

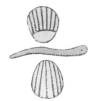

...and yelled as loudly as they could.

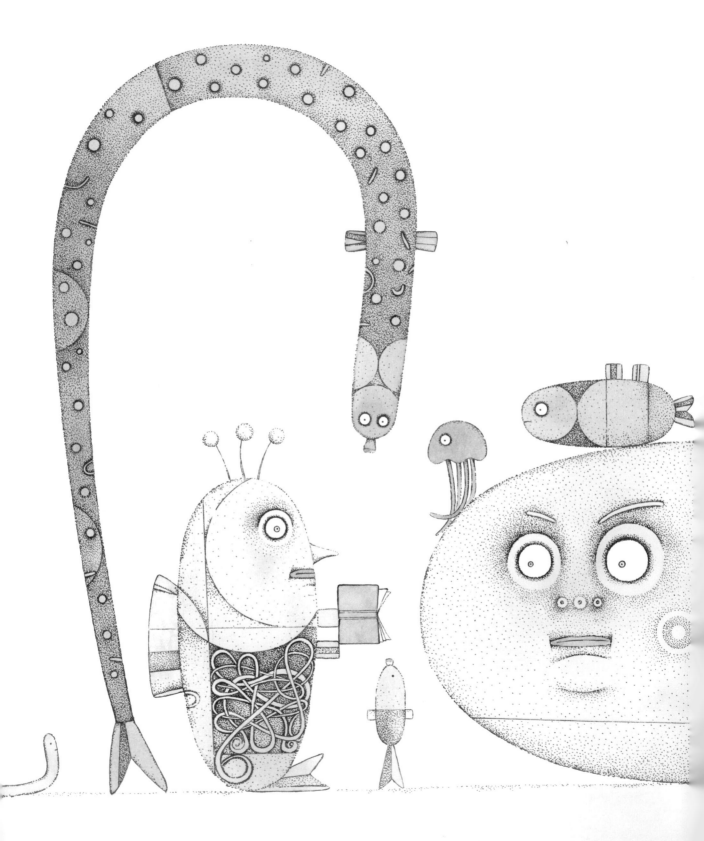

But when it was time to go to bed, the fish couldn't
fall asleep. It was as if something was missing.
Exactly! They were missing a bedtime story!

The fish examined the book, turning it over, and were
utterly clueless. You see, they could not read.

A big hungry cat noticed the fish worrying.

'Can I maybe help you?' the big hungry cat asked.

'Yes', said the fish. 'Please read to us!'

'I will gladly read to you, but only on one condition', the cat purred. 'When I have finished reading the book, you have to let me eat you!'

The fish happily agreed – so desperate they were to hear a bedtime story.

Silly fish!

And the big hungry cat started reading. It was a
beautiful story. Truly beautiful! The fishes' hearts
filled with longing and tenderness.

They suddenly remembered the Sea and all
the good times they had shared together.

Sweet Sea! Where are you? When will you be back?
The fish burst out crying.

Huge tears poured from the fishes' eyes and flowed
down their cheeks. But it wasn't just the fish that cried,
but also the starfish, turtles and worms.

There was no end to their tears. Soon enough everything was splashing and washing around them.

The big hungry cat ran away without even finishing the book.
Because cats, as we know, are afraid of getting wet.

There and then the fish noticed, that thanks to
all their tears, the Sea was all around them again!
They stopped crying at once and hugged her.

'I'm sorry I left you on your own for so long',
the Sea murmured, and finished reading the story.

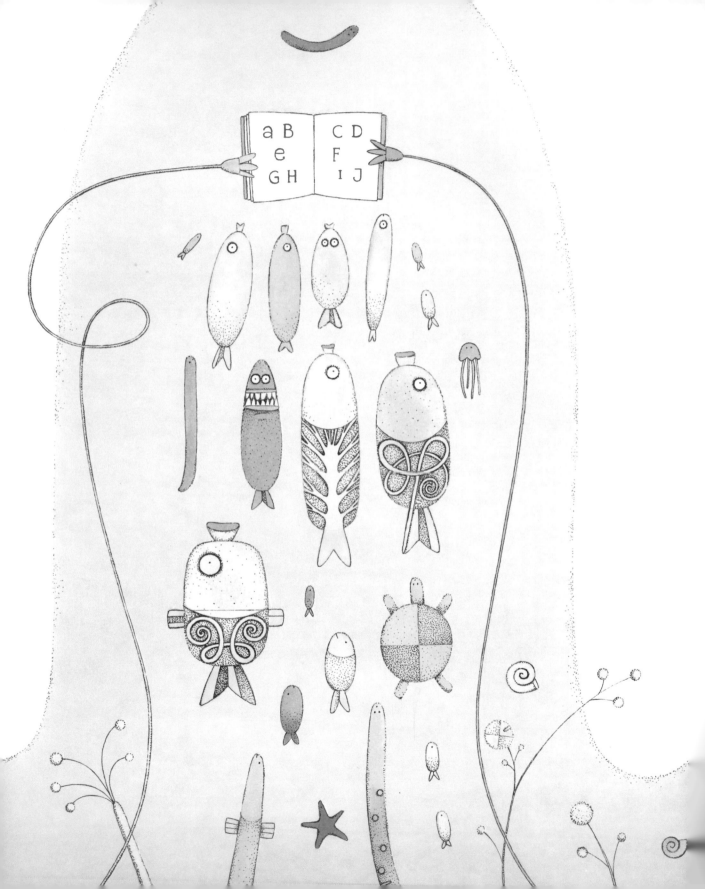

The next day, the Sea taught all her fish how to read.

'If I go away again', she told them, 'you can
now manage without me.'

And she talked at length about how good it was
for them to be educated fish.

But the fish didn't listen to her anymore –
the book was too exciting.

'What a pleasant moment!' the Sea smiled.
'A perfect time to think my own thoughts.'

First published in the United Kingdom in 2021 by
Thames & Hudson Ltd, 181A High Holborn, London WC1V 7QX

The Sea © 2021 Thames & Hudson Ltd, London
Text and Illustrations © 2021 Piret Raud

British Library Cataloguing-in-Publication Data
A catalogue record for this book is available from the British Library

ISBN 978-0-500-65213-8

Printed and bound in China by Everbest Printing Investment Ltd

FSC
www.fsc.org

MIX
Paper from
responsible sources
FSC® C124385

Be the first to know about our new releases,
exclusive content and author events by visiting
thamesandhudson.com
thamesandhudsonusa.com
thamesandhudson.com.au